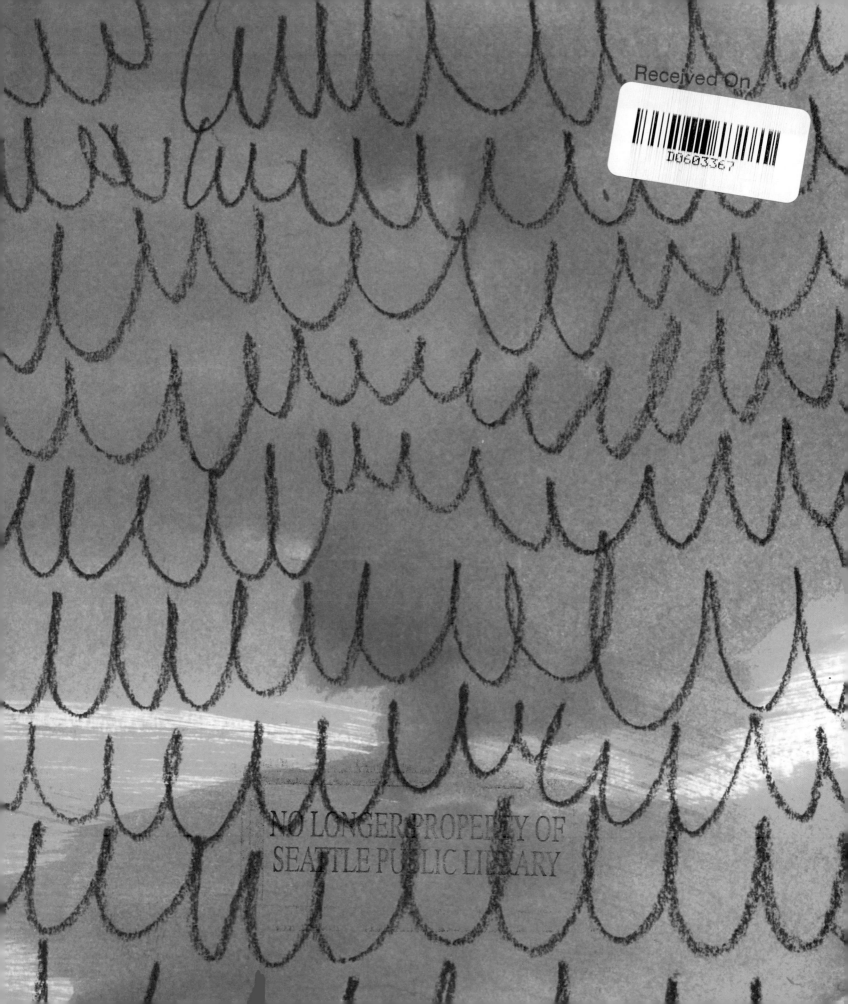

# THE WHOPPER

To my mum, who knits beautiful sweaters (honestly!)

First U.S. edition 2017

Library of Congress Catalog Card Number pending
ISBN 978-0-7636-9291-9

17 18 19 20 21 22 TLF 10 9 8 7 6 5 4 3 2 1

Printed in Dongguan, Guangdong, China

This book was typeset in Futura.
The illustrations were done in mixed media.

TEMPLAR BOOKS

an imprint of
Candlewick Press
99 Dover Street
Somerville, Massachusetts 02144
www.candlewick.com

# THE WHOPPER

Rebecca Ashdown

templar books
an imprint of Candlewick Press

Boris and Percy loved it when Grandma came to stay.
There was just one problem.
Grandma had been knitting again.

Boris liked his new sweater. Percy did *not*.
"Just right for walking the dog in!" cooed Grandma.

Walking the dog in his new sweater did make Percy feel **much** better.

Until the dog chased a cat . . .

got tangled in the bushes . . .

splashed in a puddle . . .

and rolled in something stinky.

There was only one place for the sweater now!

When they got home, it was clear something was missing.
"Percival! Where's your new sweater?" asked Mom.

"I've . . . er . . . lost it," he mumbled.

Percy felt horrible.

He had told a whopping lie.

Percy went to his room. He needed to be alone.

But then he noticed a strange creature.

"What are you?" cried Percy.

"You told a big, hairy, monstrous lie," said the creature. "It was a whopper. I am your Whopper!"

Percy showed the Whopper to his brother.
"What is *that*?" asked Boris.

"It's my lie, Boris. It's a Whopper," Percy whispered.
"And I don't know what to do with him."

The boys went downstairs. So did the Whopper.
That's when Percy discovered . . .

grown-ups couldn't see the Whopper!

When Dad asked Percy when he'd last seen his sweater,
Percy said nothing. The Whopper began to grow.

When Mom said what a shame it was that he'd lost it,
Percy said nothing. The Whopper grew bigger still.

Even when Grandma left, Percy stayed silent.
By now, the Whopper was huge!

"It won't stop growing," said Percy.
"What am I going to do?"

"There's only one thing to do," said Boris.
"You need to tell the truth."

"Never!" declared Percy.

That evening, the Whopper brushed his teeth, washed his hairy face, and climbed into bed next to Percy.

It was a very **long** night indeed.
When the Whopper woke . . .

he shouted, I'M HUNGRY!

And in one mouthful, he gobbled Percy up.

Then, the Whopper got dressed,

helped himself to breakfast,

played with the baby,

and went to school.

It was a busy day for the Whopper.

When he got home, he was hungrier than ever.

And now he was looking at Boris....

Suddenly, the Whopper opened his mouth wide.

"Stop!" came a voice from the Whopper's belly.

"Mom!
I told a lie.
It was me!
I ruined the sweater
Grandma gave me!"

Then the Whopper began to fade away.

Until with a final PLINK . . . he was gone!

"Oh, Percy!" said his mom. "Thank you for telling me the truth at last."

The next day, Percy decided to send his grandma a letter to say that he was sorry for ruining the sweater.

A week later, a **package** arrived.

Percy **loved** getting packages. There was just one problem. . . .

Grandma had been knitting *again*!

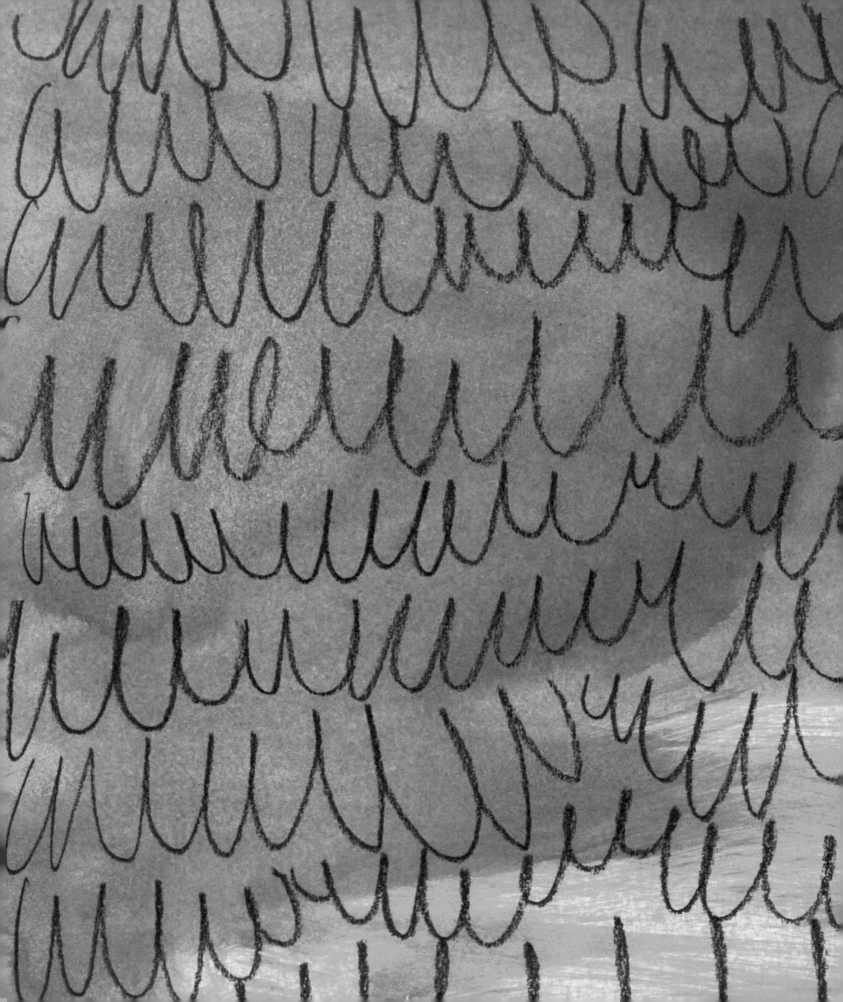